FLIP
and the
MORNING

FLIP AND THE MORNING

STORY AND PICTURES BY WESLEY DENNIS

THE VIKING PRESS · NEW YORK

To Gigi Spencer

FLIP
and the
MORNING

Flip liked to get up very early.

His mother didn't mind in summer, because Flip could play in the big field without waking her.

But in winter Flip and his mother were kept in a box stall, and when she wanted to sleep, Flip could be an awful nuisance.

And the pig, who lived under the barn, found it hard to get the extra hour of sleep that he liked with someone walking around overhead.

Even the rooster, who thought that he got up early, didn't like to be awakened by someone bumping into a water pail.

One day Willie the goat, who never liked to get up until at least ten o'clock, decided that he must do something about Flip's rising so early.

So he made up a story and told it to Flip.

It was about a spring on the farm. At this spring, he said, lived a beautiful wood duck who was very, very old and knew almost everything that there was to know.

If Flip could only find this spring, the wood duck
would be glad to share his wisdom with Flip.

"Of course," said Willie, "you must look for this spring very early in the morning because you can only find it when the rising sun is shining on it. And you must be quiet because wood ducks do not like noise."

Flip was so excited about the story of the spring and the wood duck that he could hardly wait to tell his mother. He begged her to let him go out first thing in the morning and try to find them.

His mother knew that this was just one of Willie Goat's made-up stories. But she also knew that with Flip out of the stall looking for a wood duck, she could sleep a little longer.

So she told him he could go, if he would promise to be back for breakfast.

Even before the sun was up the next morning,
Flip had jumped lightly out of the box stall,
landing on a pile of hay without making a sound.

He tiptoed out of the barn without waking a single animal.

There was just light enough for Flip to begin his hunt. He knew the spring must be well hidden or he would have seen it before.

First he headed toward the woods on the other side of the farm. That's where a wood duck would be likely to live. But he found no wood duck there.

It might be in that clump of honeysuckle. The vines were so thick that even his own mother never went there. No, no wood duck there.

Perhaps it was around that big rock pile. Flip and his mother never went there because it was all rocks and no grass. No, no wood duck there.

Next he hunted along the edge of the swamp where the cat-o'-nine-tails grew. His mother had never taken him to the swamp because there were too many mosquitoes.

All he found there was a big, ugly snapping turtle.

Flip knew no duck would live to be very, very old where HE was.

But Flip *did* find the spring, and he did talk to the wood duck, who was just as beautiful as Willie had said.

Back at the farm, all the animals were having their very best sleep since Flip had been staying in nights.

Willie the goat had just shifted sides and was looking forward to another four hours of sleep when a wild commotion was heard.

Before he was really awake he felt a terrific pull on his beard.

Flip shouted, "*I found it—I found it! I found the spring and I talked to the duck!*"

Willie started to say, "You couldn't have," but instead he said, "What did the duck have to say?"

"HE SAID FOR ME TO COME RIGHT HOME AND WAKE YOU UP. HE WANTS TO KNOW HOW—IN—THE—WORLD YOU EVER KNEW ABOUT HIM?"

MAI